A Very Clumsy Tale

by Ilanit Oliver
illustrated by Susan Hall

Ready-to-Read

Simon Spotlight
New York London Toronto Sydney

SIMON SPOTLIGHT
An imprint of Simon & Schuster Children's Publishing Division
1230 Avenue of the Americas, New York, New York 10020

For information about special discounts for bulk purchases, please contact
Simon & Schuster Special Sales at 1-866-506-1949 or business@simonandschuster.com.
Manufactured in the United States of America 0611 LAK
First Edition
2 4 6 8 10 9 7 5 3 1
ISBN 978-1-4424-2250-6
ISBN 978-1-4424-3930-6 (eBook)

I am Clumsy Smurf, and this is **my** side of the story. I guess the other side is not really wrong. But it is not my fault I am so clumsy!

It all began with the practice for the Blue Moon Festival. When I got there, the other Smurfs told me to leave!

"It is just a safety issue," Gutsy said. They thought I would do something clumsy, and somebody would get hurt!

And they were right! I knocked down the whole stage—even though I did not mean to.

"It's okay, Clumsy," Smurfette said. "Nobody is smurfect."

I ran into the forest to get smurfroot for the Smurfs who were hurt. I wanted to help, but one minute I was picking smurfroot, the next minute Gargamel and his mean cat, Azrael, were chasing me!

I jumped through the invisible shield and thought I was home free. Instead I led them to our village! I tried to get all the Smurfs to safety by heading into the forest.

But I must have taken a wrong turn because the road ended at a steep cliff.

“Clumsy, wait!” Smurfette cried.
“You are going the wrong way!”
I was able to stop in time—and
then started to fall!
“Help, Smurfette!” I called.

That's when Gutsy, Brainy, Grouchy,
and Papa arrived.

"Hold on, lad!" Gutsy yelled. "We'll form a smurf bridge to get you!"

Then Azrael and Gargamel appeared!
"You belong to me now!" the wizard growled.
Papa had no choice! "Not this time, Gargamel," he said, letting go of the stick he was holding on to.

We all fell into a portal! When we came out the other side, we were in a whole new world.
"Where the smurf are we?" Grouchy asked.
There were tall buildings, lots of people, and lots of noise!

Suddenly, Azrael appeared!
I ran as fast as I could.
I climbed up a bench and
fell into a box!

I could not smurf a thing, but I could feel the box moving. I ended up in the mushroom of Grace and Patrick Winslow, who were very nice. Luckily Grouchy, Smurfette, Gutsy, Brainy, and Papa had followed me there too.

"Master Winslow," Papa said, "there must be something about the Blue Moon on your magic box."
We knew we needed a Blue Moon to get home.

But there was nothing on Patrick's box about a Blue Moon.
"Do not worry, little Smurfs," Papa said. "I will just smurf us a potion to create a Blue Moon."

But first he needed a stargazer to make sure the stars in the sky were lined up. Brainy figured out that Patrick had one at his office, so they went—without me.

“Clumsy,” Papa said, “I think it might be best if you stay here.”

I felt awful. They did not want me to come! Deep down I knew this was all my fault—well, kind of.

If I had not gone smurfing around the forest, we would still be home. Oh, smurf! I wish I were less clumsy.

Even though I could not go with them, I still wanted to help. I decided not to eat any more smurfberries so there would be enough for everyone else.

I also decided to try to *grow* some smurfberries. If I could make them grow, maybe everyone would forgive me.
Oh, and I did not mean to knock that pot over!

Later, Grace needed help painting. I asked her if she was sure she wanted **my** help, what with me being so clumsy. She said yes! "I hate being clumsy," I told her.

"I know how you feel. I am clumsy, too," she said. "But, you can be anything you want if you are open to it. You could even be a hero."

Me? Could I really be a hero? That would be smurfy!

Just then Grace got a call from Patrick. He needed her to pick everyone up, so she and I got into a yellow wagon and went to his office. On the way back to Grace's mushroom, Gutsy spotted a stargazer!

We all ran into the store to find it. The store was filled with all kinds of strange and magical inventions—and people who could not keep their hands to themselves! They chased us around trying to catch us! It was as bad as running from Gargamel!

Good thing Papa was able to
find the stargazer and we escaped.
Papa was up all night trying to
figure out when to smurf a
Blue Moon.

In the morning, Papa had good news!
"The stars have told me when to smurf the Blue Moon. We are going home—tonight!" he cried.
But Papa still needed a special book to help him with the spell. Patrick knew just where to find this book.

I stayed back while Papa, Brainy, Gutsy, Smurfette, and Grouchy went to a bookstore. They came back with the spell, but no Papa! Gargamel had caught him!

"We cannot go home without Papa!" I cried. So we all agreed, "No Smurf left behind!"

Patrick figured out where Gargamel had taken Papa, so off we went! That's right—WE! Thanks to Grace, I finally got the chance to help. Patrick took us to the castle near where we first arrived. Then we got to work!

Gutsy and I kept Gargamel busy while Brainy smurfed a Blue Moon. The portal opened up! Brainy went back to Smurf Village and got more Smurfs to help.

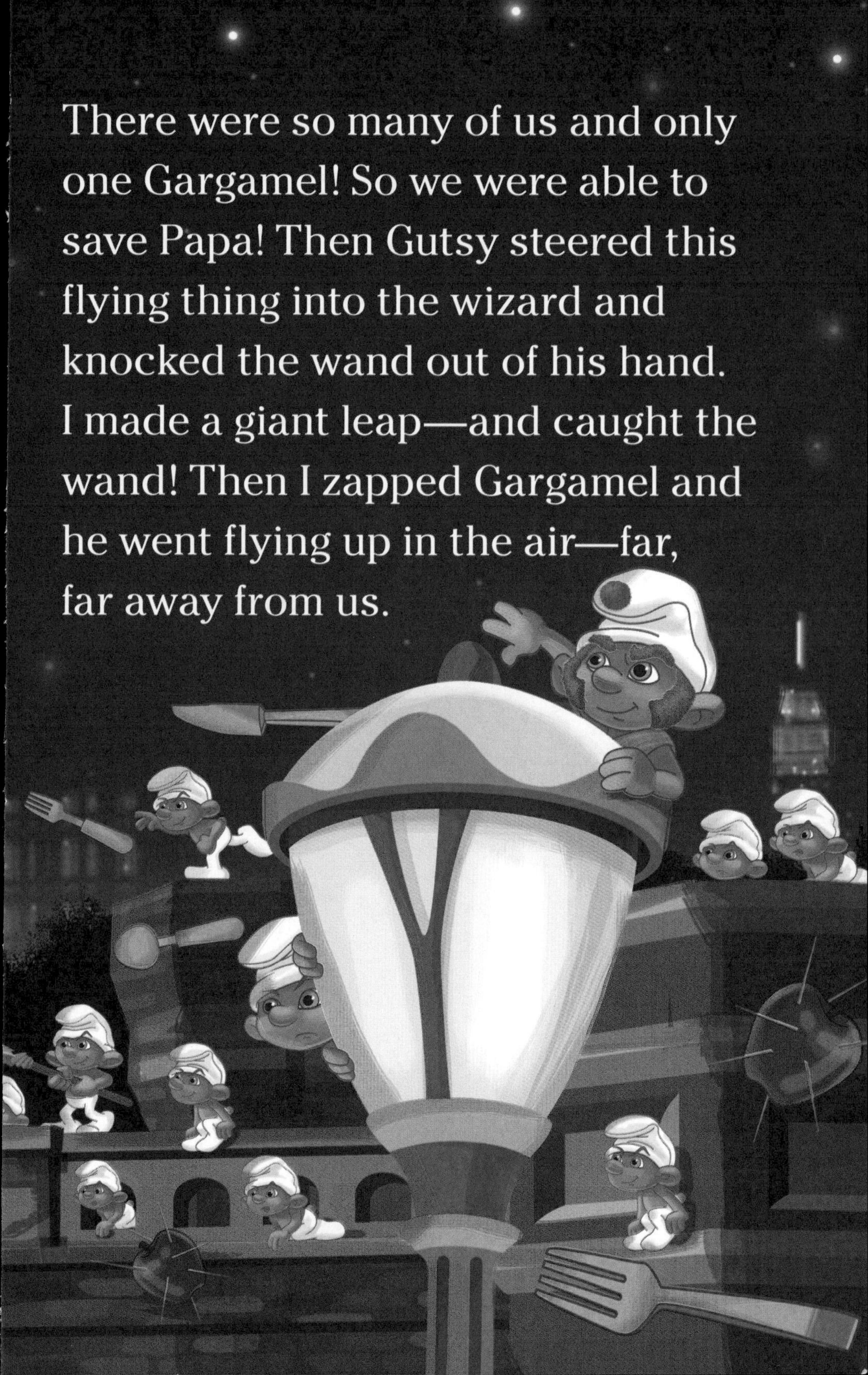

There were so many of us and only one Gargamel! So we were able to save Papa! Then Gutsy steered this flying thing into the wizard and knocked the wand out of his hand. I made a giant leap—and caught the wand! Then I zapped Gargamel and he went flying up in the air—far, far away from us.

"Clumsy! Clumsy!" everyone chanted. We were free, Papa was safe, and we were on our way home! Grace was right. I may be Clumsy, but I am now a hero, too!